NORWOOD HOUSE PRESS

Wonderful Weather

By Kathleen Corrigan

Search for Sounds
Consonants:
f, l, m, n, r, s, x

Scan this code to access the Teacher's Notes for this series or visit
www.norwoodhousepress.com/decodables

DEAR CAREGIVER, *The Decodables* series contains books following a systematic, cumulative phonics scope and sequence aligned with the science of reading. Each book in the *Search for Sounds* series allows its reader to apply their phonemic awareness and phonics knowledge in engaging and relatable texts. The keywords within each text have been carefully selected to allow readers to identify pictures beginning with sounds and letters they have been explicitly taught.

When reading these books with your child, encourage them to isolate the beginning sound in the keywords, find the corresponding picture, and identify the letter that makes the beginning sound by pointing to the letter placed in the corner of each page. Rereading the texts multiple times will allow your child the opportunity to build their letter sound fluency, a skill necessary for decoding.

You can be confident you are providing your child with opportunities to build their foundational decoding abilities which will encourage their independence as they become lifelong readers.

Happy Reading!

Emily Nudds, M.S. Ed Literacy
Literacy Consultant

3

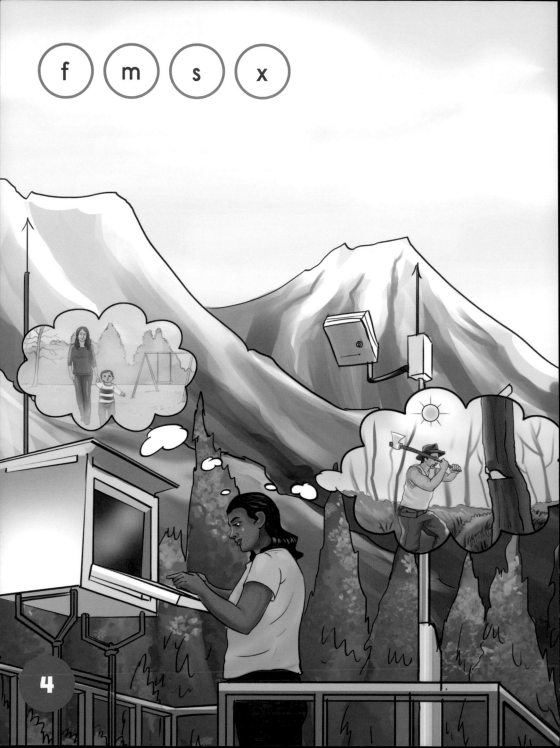

10

11

HOW TO USE THIS BOOK

Read this text with your child as they engage with each page. Then, read each keyword and ask them to isolate the beginning sound before finding the corresponding picture in the illustration. Encourage finding and pointing to the corresponding letter in the corner of the page. Additional reinforcement activities can be found in the Teacher's Notes.

Wonderful Weather
f, l, r, s

Pages 2 and 3	What do you think of when you hear the word weather?
	Rain? Snow? Sunny days? Weather is what the air and sky are like outside of our homes and buildings. The weather can be wet messy things like rain or snow, but it can also be the temperature. Temperature tells us how warm it is outside. Is it hot? Is it freezing? Is it just right? The weather can also cause amazing sights and sounds like beautiful rainbows or flashes of lightening and crashes of thunder.
	Wind is another important part of the weather. Wind is air moving across the Earth. Sometimes the wind is soft and gentle. Other times it is very fast and powerful.
	We think about the weather every day. It helps us know what to wear when we go outside. It helps grownups decide when to do certain jobs or to go different places. Weather is all around us!

Keywords: flower, fog, lamp, lightning, rain, rainbow, rug, sky, snow, snowman, snowsuit, sunny

f, m, s, x

Pages 4 and 5

Meteorologists are the scientists who study and learn about the weather. They use different tools to see what is happening high in the sky. Then they forecast or say what they think the weather will be. They may forecast a sunny day or a rainy day, or they may tell us there will be mist in the morning. Meteorologists also forecast the temperature so we know if it will be freezing or warm.

Many meteorologists have a weather box that holds some of the weather tools.

Some meteorologists are weather forecasters on TV or on the Internet. They show people what they think will happen that night and the next day. They also forecast the weather for each day of the week from Monday to Sunday.

Forecasters tell people when it is very foggy or if big storms are coming so people can be safe. You don't want to be outside in a big storm. You and your grownups can get ready if the meteorologists say a storm is coming.

Keywords: axe, box, foggy, forecaster, forest, man, meteorologist, mist, mother, mountain, snow, storm, sun, sunny, swings, symbol

Read this text with your child as they engage with each page. Then, read each keyword and ask them to isolate the beginning sound before finding the corresponding picture in the illustration. Encourage finding and pointing to the corresponding letter in the corner of the page. Additional reinforcement activities can be found in the Teacher's Notes.

f, m, r, s

Pages 6 and 7	Do you wear your swimsuit to build a snowman? No? Why not? Do you wear your snowsuit to swim at the beach? No? Why not? Do you use your umbrella to shovel snow? No? Why not? Children and grownups must think about the weather when they decide what to wear or do.
	Some clothing helps us keep warm. We wear mittens and fluffy hats. We wear jackets and thick socks. We want our skin to be cozy.
	Other clothing helps us stay cool and can protect us from the sun. We wear sunhats and shorts or swimsuits and T-shirts. We want our skin to be cool in the air and safe from the hot sun.
	We have special tools we use when the weather is messy, too. Some grownups drive snowplows or snowblowers to move heavy snow. Some grownups use snow shovels to clear it away.
	People use umbrellas and waterproof clothing to keep dry when it rains. Many children who live in rainy places have rain boots, raincoats, and rainhats. Fishermen who work hard on the ocean have rain clothes, too.

Keywords: fish, fishermen, man, mittens, mom, rain boots, raincoats, rainhats, skin, snow, snowblower, snowman, snowplow, sprinkler, street, sun, sunhats, sunscreen, swimsuit

f, m, n, x

Pages 8 and 9

Animals find ways to be safe when the weather changes. Many animals make nests in trees. Nuthatches and other birds may huddle in their nests when it rains. Other animals, like some squirrels, make nests high in trees, too. The branches help keep the bad weather away.

Some animals, like mink, build dens in logs to stay dry and warm. They can live in them all year long. A fox will dig a den, too. They are cozy in their dens. Leaves can be a good shelter for small animals that want to stay dry and hidden.

Other animals make their nests under the ground. Moles dig tunnels. They put grass in their tunnels to make nests. This keeps them safe from bad weather and other animals.

Some animals like rainy weather and they don't have to hide. Flamingos and frogs think rain is fun.

Keywords: flamingos, fox, frog, mink, mole, nest, nuthatche

m, n

Page 10

Many animals must protect themselves from winter weather. Some, like monarch butterflies and mourning doves, migrate to warm places to get away from the freezing snow. This means they fly a very long way to a winter home. Then, in the spring, they fly back.

Other animals crawl into a den or hole and sleep through the winter. They stay out of the snow and sleet. Marmots are furry animals that often live around mountains. A big family of marmots will crawl into their cozy nest in October and won't come out for at least six months!

Some newts sleep all winter in nests under logs, in leaf piles, or in holes.

Keywords: marmot, monarch butterflies, mountains, mourning doves, nest, newt

Read this text with your child as they engage with each page. Then, read each keyword and ask them to isolate the beginning sound before finding the corresponding picture in the illustration. Encourage finding and pointing to the corresponding letter in the corner of the page. Additional reinforcement activities can be found in the Teacher's Notes.

f, l, r, s, x	
Page 11	Animals must be careful of the sun, too. Wild animals don't have sunhats or sunscreen, but they have ways to stay safe.
	Some reptiles, like snakes and lizards, hide under rocks or in holes when it is very hot. Many fish will swim down to cooler water when it gets too hot. They will swim back up later in the day.
	People wear warm clothes in the winter and put on cooler clothes in the summer. Many furry animals change their clothes, too. Rabbits and foxes are two of the animals that shed their winter fur for lighter summer fur. A fox who is shedding his fur has a very messy coat.
	Changing weather is part of life. People and animals have all learned ways to enjoy the weather and be safe, too.

Keywords: fish, flowers, fox, fur, lizard, log, rabbit, rocks, snake, sun, sunny, swim

Norwood House Press • www.norwoodhousepress.com
The Decodables ©2024 by Norwood House Press. All Rights Reserved.
Printed in the United States of America.
367N—O82023

Library of Congress Cataloging-in-Publication Data has been filed and is available at catalog.loc.gov

Literacy Consultant: Emily Nudds, M.S.Ed Literacy
Editorial and Production Development and Management: Focus Strategic Communications Inc.
Editors: Christine Gaba, Christi Davis-Martell
Illustration Credit: Mindmax, Tranistics
Covers: Shutterstock, Macrovector

Hardcover ISBN: 978-1-68450-724-5   Paperback ISBN: 978-1-68404-862-5
eBook ISBN: 978-1-68404-921-9